© 1997 Geddes & Grosset Ltd
Published by Geddes & Grosset Ltd,
New Lanark, Scotland.

ISBN 1 85534 860 8

Produced by Simon Girling & Associates,
Hadleigh, Suffolk.

Printed and bound in China.

10 9 8 7 6 5 4 3 2 1

Meet New
Neighbours

GEDDES & GROSSET

The house next door had been empty for
a long time. Old Mrs Sinclair, who used to
live there, had moved away to live with
her daughter. A sign had gone up at the
gate, which said, "For Sale", and

Susie and Sam had watched lots of
people coming and going, looking at the
house. Then one day the "For Sale" sign
was taken down.

Susie and Sam wondered who had bought the house.

"I hope a boy comes to live next door," said Sam.

"I want a girl to play with," said Susie.

"You'll soon find out who our new neighbours will be," said Mum. "They will be moving in very soon."

The next Friday, early in the morning, a great big removal van drew up outside the house next door. All morning, four men trudged back and forth from the van

to the house, carrying furniture and boxes.

Susie and Sam watched them out of the window.

"Are they going to be living next door?" asked Susie.

"Don't be silly," said Sam, "They are only the removal men!"

"Then who is going to be living next door?" asked Susie.

"You'll just have to wait and see," said Mum.

"I've counted four beds," said Sam. "One big one, like the one you and Dad have, and three little ones. Do you think that's a clue?"

"I don't know," said Mum. She laughed. "I'm not a very good detective!"

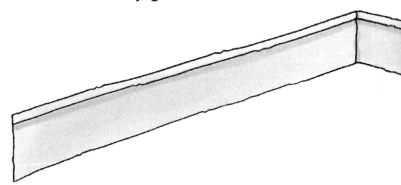

Later on that day, a little red car arrived next door. A woman and a man, dressed in old jeans and T-shirts, got out and went into the house. The removal men stopped work for a little while and sat on the pavement beside the van, eating sandwiches and drinking tea. Then on they went, fetching and carrying, back and forth.

15

"Well, we've seen a woman and a man, but still no children," said Sam. "What a pity. I thought we might get someone to play with."

"Wait a minute," said Susie. "Look at what the removal men are carrying in now—a swing!"

"Grown-ups playing on swings? Very strange!" said Sam.

"Come and have your tea now," said Mum. "We'll leave them to get settled in and then perhaps tomorrow we can go round and introduce ourselves."

Next morning, Mum baked a cake as a welcome present for the new neighbours. Sam sniffed the smell of baking in the kitchen. "Do you remember the oatmeal biscuits that Mrs Sinclair used to make, when she lived next door?" he said. "I miss her!"

"I'm sure the new neighbours will be very nice, biscuits or no biscuits," said Mum. She put the cake in a tin. Then they went next door and rang the doorbell.

It was the woman who answered.

"How kind of you!" she said when she saw the cake. "My name is Cheryl Armitage, but you must all call me Cherrie. My husband, Stan, has just gone off to fetch the children from their grandmother's house. They stayed there during the move."

"So that's why you have a swing," said Sam. "You have children!"

"I certainly do," said Cherrie. "Jenny is nine, Sophie is six and John is five. They'll be here soon, so why don't you come in and wait for them. Then we can all have some cake!"

21

The house was full of boxes and piles of all sorts of stuff, but Cherrie found places for everyone to sit. Then the front door opened, and a man and three children came in. The children all had fair hair and blue eyes.

"Hello!" they all said together. Cherrie gave them each a hug.

"Jenny, Sophie and John, I'd like you to meet your new friends from next door—Susie and Sam!"

Susie and Sam felt a little bit shy, seeing three strange faces smiling at them. Susie went and stood very close to Mum. Cherrie laughed.

"Let's all have some cake and get to know each other. Then the children can explore the house and garden together," she said.

Susie and Sam stayed there all morning. They helped John and Sophie and Jenny to sort out the toys in their new rooms. Then they all built a den out of

packing boxes in the garden. Mum stayed too, to help Cherrie and Stan with the unpacking. Then they all went back to Susie and Sam's house for lunch.

Susie and Sam did not take long to decide that they were very pleased with their new neighbours. At the end of the day, Sam had just one question.

"I wonder if Cherrie can make oatmeal biscuits?" he said.

"Oh, Sam!" said Mum.